The Adventures of Celtic: "Going for the Gold"

AuthorHouse™
1663 Liberty Drive
Bloomington, IN 47403
www.authorhouse.com
Phone: 1 (800) 839-8640

Published by AuthorHouse 02/19/2015

ISBN: 978-1-4969-7187-6 (SC)
ISBN: 978-1-4969-7188-3 (E)

Library of Congress Control Number: 2015934125

Print information available on the last page.

This book is printed on acid-free paper.

Illustrations by: Dan Drewes

authorHOUSE®

Every so often, my family lets me ride in the car with them. It's usually a trip to grandmas or a quick jaunt to Sonic for apple slices. But, sometimes, I have to go see the veterinarian.

I don't like the vet. All we have to do is pull up in front of the vet's office and I fall apart faster than our cat Rusty does when I decide to pounce on his head.

"Noooooo," I howled the other day as Dad stopped the car in front of the vet and Colton tried to drag me out of the back seat.

"I don't like this place," I barked. "It smells like Holly's breath in there."

Holly is a black cat who hangs out in our house. She is mean and always smells like stale catnip.

I tried to hold my ground in the back seat, but Colton finally was able to hook the leash to my dog collar and drag me into the doctor's office. Dad was talking to a couple of women in white coats while I huddled near Colton and started shaking like a leaf.

"It's all right, boy," he said, trying his best to console me.

I looked at him, tilted my head and barked: "Are you nuts? They are about to stretch my legs, pull my ears and stick needles in the back side of my body. I don't want any part of it."

Unfortunately, I didn't have a choice.

The first step was the scale. I had never had to worry about my weight. But, ever since Dad and Tyler started letting me lick their plates, I have noticed my collar getting a little tight.

"32 pounds," the nurse grumbled.

Wow, I thought to myself. I have really grown up in two years. No wonder Rusty cries when I jump on him.

Then, Dad and I were sent into a tiny office. That was OK until three nurses walked in together. I jumped up on the chair with Dad, put both my front paws around his neck and hung on for dear life.

The nurses laughed.

"It is OK," one of the ladies said. "We aren't going to hurt you."

Yea, right, I thought. This place is like the doggy torture chamber. And I knew there was no way out.

"Come here, boy," one of the nurses said as she tried to pull me off Dad's neck. "We need to check you out and give you a shot so you don't get sick."

The thought of the shot made me sick.

"Noooo," I howled.

But they stuck me with the needle anyway. Surprisingly, it didn't hurt. And they were all patting me on the head for being such a good puppy.

"I wish all of our patients were this good," the nurses said as they started to leave the room.

I was pretty proud of myself. My tail was wagging. I started kissing Dad on the cheek. I just knew he was going to take me for an ice cream cone after this performance.

"Mr. Hveem," one of the nurses said before she left, "there is just one thing. I wouldn't say Celtic is overweight, but we don't want him to gain any more weight. He needs to get in shape."

Get in shape? Look at this figure. My hind legs are strong. My chest is large. There is not an ounce of fat on me. I am Celtic!

"Did you hear that, C," Dad said. "No more licking our plates. You are in training."

Special Diet

I found out the first part about being "in training" was being on a special diet.

I could still eat the cats' food when they weren't looking. And carrots, apple slices and tuna were still on the menu. But there was no more licking plates at night, and my gigantic food bag now had a different color on it.

"I decided to get the healthy dog food for Celtic instead of the normal food," I heard "The Mama" tell Dad after she got home from the grocery store. "It has less fat."

There is that word again. Fat. Surely, they aren't calling me fat. Look at me. I should be the poster puppy for fitness. Heck, the only thing my body needs is a good haircut. My beard is starting to look like Abe Lincoln's.

"I think that is a good idea," Dad said to The Mama. "The vet said he is not overweight, he just can't gain any more weight."

I looked at Dad and laughed.

"Dad, you need to be eating this food a lot more than I do," I thought. "You are overweight."

But I love Dad. He plays tug with me more than anyone else in the family. He laughs at me all the time. He is very loud when he laughs. And he lets me sleep under the covers with him when the rest of the family is on vacation. I have to. Dad keeps the house colder than the North Pole.

"I think we should limit the number of bones we give Celtic, too," Dad said. "I think those things are pretty fattening."

Wait a minute, I thought. Low-fat dog food is one thing. Limiting bones is quite another. I have bones stashed all over the house and back yard in case of emergency. I immediately started searching for them. This was definitely an emergency.

"I think a couple bones a day are OK," The Mama said. "They are pretty little."

I went up and started kissing The Mama. She always has been my favorite. She is so beautiful. I wanted to let her know how much I appreciated her. So I piddled on the floor. Some habits are hard to break.

"CELTIC," the Mama yelled. "What are we going to do with you?"

"You can start by taking me off this special diet," I barked.

Running with Zach

"The Mama" and Dad are pretty good about taking me for walks around the neighborhood at night. But after the nurses at the vet decided I needed to get in shape, my oldest brother, Zachary, decided he wanted me to start running.

"Say, what?" I barked.

My grandpa, Joe, likes to run and ride a bike. But this was the first I had heard of Zach going on a run.

"Come on C," Zach said one day when he was home from college. "You want to go on a…"

For some reason, every time I hear "You want to go…," I start to go crazy. I know they are going to ask "You want to go on a walk." I don't have to hear "on a walk." But this time I should have listened. I saw Zach stretching his legs in the kitchen. My family never stretches before a walk.

"OK, C," he said. "Let's see if you can keep up with me."

I laughed. I wanted to say, "Let's see if you can keep up with me." But then again, I thought we were just going on a walk.

The minute we stepped off the front porch, Zach took off running while holding my leash. I was so excited. I was half running and half jumping. I wanted to bite my leash in two so I could break free and show Zach how fast I could really go.

"Stop it, Celtic," Zach said as he continued to jog along the street. "You are going to get all tangled up."

I didn't care. I love to run. This was fun. But it also was hot on the old paws. And Zach didn't seem to be ready to stop anytime soon.

"We are going to get you in shape, C," Zach said as he started to pull up alongside me. "I am going to be coming home a lot on weekends to work, so I will take you running."

By this time, my tongue was almost touching the ground as I panted to keep up with Zach. It was 100 degrees outside. Couldn't we have picked a better time to get in shape?

"How are you doing, C-Dog," Zach asked as we circled back around the pond at the end of our street.

I couldn't tell him I was ready to faint, so I let out a big "Rup."

"Good, boy," he said. "We are almost home."

Thank God, I thought. I was about ready to have heat stroke.

We walked in the front door and The Mama could tell we were tired. Zach was sweating up a storm and I made a mad dash for the water bowl.

"How far did you run?" The Mama asked Zach.

"A little over one mile," Zach said. "Celtic did pretty good. He was ahead of me most of the way."

I walked over to my favorite chair and plopped down like my Aunt Chris does in her Doggy Bed. I was exhausted. But I also felt very excited. This getting in shape stuff might be OK. I just needed to find a couple bones so I could make it until dinner.

Learning to swim

It's a common fact that most dogs know how to swim the minute they are born. Well, not really swim, but paddle. That is why they call it "Dog Paddle." But if I was ever going to get in shape, I needed to learn how to swim the right way.

At least that is what Tyler told me.

"Celtic," said my favorite 9-year-old boy, "We are going to teach you how to swim like we do. We are going to go to Aunt Sally's pool and I am going to give you lessons. That will get you in good shape."

I didn't really know what "lessons" were, but I was excited about going to Aunt Sally's. I knew Benny and Frankie lived there. I knew they had a big bouncy thing to jump on. And I knew there were plenty of frogs, lizards and squirrels to chase in the back yard.

Aunt Sally also had a swimming pool where I could cool off after running around like a rooster with a bucket over its head.

"Celtic," Tyler yelled to me a couple days later, "it is time to go to Aunt Sally's. We are going to start your swim lessons today."

There was that word again. Lessons. What the heck are lessons? I knew it had to do with swimming, but I didn't know it meant teach me how to swim. Heck, I already knew how to swim. Or so I thought.

"OK, C," Tyler said as we got into Aunt Sally's pool. "First, we have to put your goggles on."

Tyler grabbed my stomach, slipped this leather string over my ears and then placed the plastic pieces on the end of the leather string over my eyes. I thought he was crazy. But the minute I put my face in the water, I could see everything.

"Woo, Hoo," I barked as I bobbed up and down while doggy paddling around the pool. "This is the bomb."

Tyler laughed. Then he grabbed me and took me to the side of the pool.

"Celtic, you have to learn to do the crawl stroke if you really want to get in shape," he said. "You put your face in the water and then make circle motions with your front paws and kick with your back paws."

He put me in the water face first and I tried to bring my front paws over my head one at a time. My elbows kept bopping me on top of the head.

"C," Tyler yelled. "You have to keep your front paws straight."

Yea, right, I thought to myself. But I wanted to please Tyler, so I managed to keep them straight enough to keep my elbows from hitting my head. I also started to kick my back paws at the same time. I looked like a frog caught in a fish tank.

"Help," I barked to Tyler as I was slowly going under the water. "I am stuck in a whirlpool."

Tyler grabbed me and rolled me over on my back. Funny thing was, I didn't stop moving my front paws or back paws. And now I could swim! I was back stroking all over the pool.

"That's it, C," Tyler screamed. "You have got it."

I didn't know what I had, but I know I still had my goggles on. It was so foggy I couldn't see a thing. But I had learned to swim. I couldn't wait to hear what the vet had to say about this.

Pumping Iron

After learning how to swim, I practically begged my family to fill up "The Mama's" hot tub, turn on the water jets and let me backstroke around the miniature pool.

I would sneak into the laundry room, find the pool bag and then dig through the bag until I found my goggles. I would flip the goggles on my head and then go sit by the hot tub.

"I want to swim," I would howl.

My family would laugh and laugh. Every now and then, they would even fill up the garden-sized tub and throw me in. I was in heaven. I would even bring a few bones into the tub just in case I got hungry.

But that came to a stop when Zachary came home from college again. Besides running, Zach is really into lifting weights. I guess he decided I needed to lift weights, too.

"C," he said, "If you are going to get in shape, you have to get stronger. The only way to get stronger is to lift weights."

I saw the weights Zachary lifted in the garage. He put two 35-pound circle things on both ends of a long metal bar and then lifted the weight up and down while he was lying down.

That was not for me.

"No way," I yelled at Zach as I sprinted into my crate.

He just walked away and started building a little weight set. He tied a tuna can on each end of a ruler and brought it to me. Naturally, I tried to lift it up with my teeth. No such luck.

"Come here, C," Zach said.

I ambled over. I knew there was no way I was going to get to eat this tuna until I did what Zach said.

"OK; now what," I barked.

Zach rolled me over on my back and started rubbing my belly. I love belly rubs. In fact, I love them so much that all four of my paws stick straight up in the air. I become almost paralyzed.

My brother, of course, knew what I would do. Once he saw my paws in the air, he put the ruler in my front paws. I had to admit, I felt like Harley, the big German Shepard up the street.

"What do I do know," I whimpered.

"Just slowly let the ruler down to your chest, then push it back up as far as you can," Zach said. "Come on Celtic. Do you want to get in shape or not?"

Hey, I thought. This was never my idea in the first place. But I do love to show off for my family. And I really wanted to eat this tuna, so I slowly let the ruler down to my chest. I couldn't pick it back up. Then it rolled up on my neck.

"Help," I yelped to Zach. "I am going to be a tuna sandwich."

Zach laughed, but he didn't remove the ruler. He just helped me lift it back over my head.

"There you go, Celtic," he said as he tried to contain his laughter. "Now, you have nine more to go."

Say, what?

I tried to do it again. The bar fell right on my chest. But on the third try, I was able to let it down slow, and lift it back up over my head.

"All right, C!" Zach yelled. "You are going to be one lean, mean, barking machine!"

Before long, I could do 10 reps up and over my head. I could feel my muscles starting to get stronger. I couldn't believe it. I was actually getting in shape. But I still was starving.

Riding in Style

About a year ago, Tyler built a basket on the front of his bike so I could ride with him to Great Burger. The basket lasted only half-way as I fell through on our way home.

This year, Colton had a better idea. He wanted to build me a bicycle and teach me how to ride it to Great Burger.

"Celtic," said my 18-year-old brother, who was about to go off to college with Zach. "You have to learn how to ride a bike. That way, you will be able to go with Tyler when he rides his bike, and Mom and Dad when they ride on the tandem bike."

I was all for spending more time with Tyler. He is so much fun. And I would love to show off for "The Mama." She has the most perfect laugh. But riding a bicycle? You have got to be kidding me.

"Come out here C," Colton said as he got out of the car one day. "I have something for you."

I barked at the front door and sprinted out when Tyler opened the door. When I got to the car, I saw Colton holding the smallest bicycle I had ever seen in my life. It had three wheels, a tilted skateboard seat and pedals on the front of skateboard.

"This is your bike," Colton said.

OK, I thought. But how in the world am I going to ride that thing?

"I got a really long seat that will allow you to lie down when you ride," Colton said. "While you lie down, you can pedal with your front paws, and wrap your back paws around the back of the seat."

He should have bought me a surfboard. In fact, it kind of looked like Zach's snowboard, only it was a miniature version with wheels. But I had to admit, it looked like fun.

"OK, Celtic, come over here and lie down on the bike," Colton said.

I always do what Colton says. He is very stern. I know I have to listen to him or I will be in big trouble.

"All right," I barked. "What next?"

"Put your front paws on the pedals and wrap your back paws around the back of the seat. The back wheel will help balance you as you pedal with your front paws."

I put my paws on the pedals, but I didn't know what to do next.

Colton thought for a minute, and then shouted: "Act like you are swimming."

So I started doing the crawl stroke. It worked. In no time, my bike was zipping down the street.

"Wow," Colton screamed. "You are flying, C."

I was flying. But I did not know how to steer or stop this crazy thing.

"You have to lean your body the way you want to go," yelled Colton.

I didn't know what that meant. But a couple seconds later, I almost lost my balance to the left. My bike turned perfectly to the left.

"I got it now," I barked with glee.

But I still needed to stop.

"You have to pedal backwards to put on the brake," Colton screamed.

I didn't understand.

"Just like the backstroke," he yelled.

I started to turn my paws in the opposite direction. My bike came to a stop right on command.

"You are one smart puppy," Colton said.

I don't know about that. But in a short time, I had learned to run, swim, lift weights and ride a bike. I couldn't wait to spread the word about my success.

Neighborhood Gossip

I was so excited about all of the things my brothers taught me that I couldn't wait to tell the other dogs in the neighborhood - namely, Ziggy, Harley, Parker and Coby. The five of us had become pretty close since our late-night road trip to Grandma's house. I am sure they would be so proud of me for learning how to get in shape.

But there was one problem. We were never outside at the same time. "The Mama" and Dad always take me for a walk after it gets dark so the hot cement doesn't burn my paws. Ziggy and Harley go for walks in the morning. Coby and Parker just chill out and watch cartoons.

But one day, I saw Coby and Parker's parents outside talking. Then, I saw Coby and Parker lying in the grass next to each other. I started barking at the front door.

"Let me oooouttt," I screamed.

Tyler put my leash on me and took me outside. I ran over to Coby and Parker and started talking as fast as I could.

"I went to the vet a few weeks ago," I said. "They said I couldn't gain any more weight, so I was put on this special diet and made to exercise. Since then, I have learned to run, swim, pump iron and ride a bike."

Coby and Parker looked at each other and yawned.

"Tell someone who cares," Parker said. "We are too old for that nonsense."

"Yea," added Coby, "you should tell Ziggy. She is the one who is into all that staying in shape stuff."

I turned around and was a little disappointed at their reaction. But then I saw Harley and his dad walking down the street.

"Hey, Harley," I barked as I ran toward the leader of the Hidden Lake Hounds. "I have something to tell you."

Harley stopped and I repeated the same story I told Coby and Parker.

"Listen C," Harley said in his best military voice. "I am proud of you. But I am more into marching in a straight line and behaving for my master. You should talk to Ziggy."

I know, I know, I thought. Ziggy can catch a Frisbee, jump over a six-foot fence, run like the wind and swim faster than the other dogs on the block combined.

"Tyler, we have to go down to Ziggy's," I said.

Tyler turned me around and we headed toward Ziggy's house at the end of the street. About half-way there, Ziggy came bounding out of the backyard. She was jumping up in the air and catching a tennis ball. Wow, she was so athletic.

"Ziggy," I screamed.

Ziggy saw me and stopped trying to catch the ball. She wandered over and I shared all of my accomplishments with her.

"Celtic," she said. "You should enter the Doggy Triathlon down at North Shore Park. It is next Saturday. I participate in it every year."

"What is a Doggy Triathlon," I asked.

"They have a swim, bike and running race all rolled into one," Ziggy said. "It is so much fun."

It sounded like a blast. But I could never beat Ziggy.

"The race is divided into two divisions," Ziggy said. "One division is for bigger dogs like me, and another is for smaller dogs, like you."

That was perfect. If I didn't have to compete against Ziggy, I just might have a chance to win. And I like to win.

"I am going to do it," I told Ziggy.

"Great," Ziggy said. "You better keep training. There are a lot of talented dogs out there."

I am sure there are, I thought. But I am Celtic.

Anticipation...

Once I told Tyler about the Doggy Triathlon, my whole family became excited about the competition.

"You have to train extra hard this week," Colton said.

"But not too hard," added Dad. "You want to have something left for the day of the race."

"Yes," The Mama said. "You can't be too tired or you won't be able to do your best."

"Yea, C," Tyler concluded. "We want you to win."

My head was spinning with all these suggestions. I just wanted to compete. My whole family is very competitive. But I might be the most competitive one of all.

If I see Holly jump on "The Mama's" lap, I have to kick her off and sit on "The Mama's" lap.

If Tyler runs up the stairs as fast he can, I have to zip right past him and beat him to the top.

If Colton has a girl over to the house, I can't let her sit too close to him. I have to nuzzle right in between them.

And if I see Dad take a bag of chips to the couch, I have to sit right next to him until he starts to share. Come to think of it, that is how I got here in the first place.

"I am ready for the race now," I told Tyler. "I don't know if I can wait another week."

To take my mind off the race, Tyler took me for a swim. I was amazed at how adept I had become at swimming backwards. I know it looked funny, but man, I had to look like one of those guys in the Olympics.

"C," Tyler said, "The swim is the first event in the Doggy Triathlon. It is important for you to get off to a good start."

No sweat, I thought. I will be so far ahead, the only thing those other mutts will see is the waves from my tail.

The next day, Colton took me on a bike ride. I had the pedaling down pat. But I had to be careful not to lean too much one way or the other or I would go skidding across the pavement.

"Celtic," Colton said. "When you are done with the swim, I will have your bike waiting. I will help you on, and then you are on your own. This three-wheeler is made for speed. Just stay balanced and you will dog them all."

I tilted my head.

"Dog them all? What the heck was that? Aren't we all dogs?"

The next day, my grandpa came over and said he wanted to take me "on a little run." A "little run" to me is around the block. To Grandpa Joe, it is around the world.

"Come on, Celtic," he said as he had a big smile on his face. "We are going to run sprints. We have to build up your legs so you have enough left for a big kick at the end of the race."

Grandpa took me to the same field where Colton practiced football. He told me we were going to stand at one end of the field and sprint as fast as we could to the big fork at the other end.

"No problem," I barked. "I am very fast."

I sprinted to the other end and turned around. Grandpa still had half of the field to go.

"Come on, old man," I barked.

Joe came to the big fork and said we had to line up and run back to the fork at the other end of the field as fast as we could. Once again, I left him in my doggy dust.

Then we did it again.

And again

And again.

By the time we were done, I was lying on my back under one of the forks while Grandpa was still running.

"It isn't all about being the fastest in this competition," Grandpa said. "It is about who is in the best shape."

"Yea, yea," I barked. "I am doing what Dad said. I am saving it for the race."

The Race

When we arrived at North Shore Park for the "Doggy Triathlon," I couldn't believe the number of dogs who were signed up to compete in the competition.

"I didn't think there would be this many dogs here," I turned and barked to Tyler. "I am kind of worried."

"Don't worry about it, C," Tyler said. "You are ready. You have had great training and, regardless of what Grandpa says, you are in shape. Just stay focused and you will do fine."

The dogs were separated into two groups - those who weighed more than 50 pounds and those who weighed less than 50 pounds. I went with the little group and started to size up the competition.

"Look at that guy over there," I thought as I gazed at what looked like a bulldog on steroids. "He is built like a brick house. Man, he is going to be tough to beat."

"Don't worry about him," Colton said. "All those muscle dogs are going to have a hard time with the swim. You should dust him in the water."

Yea, I thought. He will cramp up before he gets halfway across.

Then another dog zipped by. He looked like a smaller version of Ziggy. Now, I was really worried.

"What about him?" I asked Tyler. "I don't think he has an ounce of fat on him. He looks like he could run and swim forever without getting tired."

"Yea," Tyler agreed. "But I'll bet he doesn't have a bike like yours, C. You are going to blow him away in the bike ride."

The race consisted of a 500-yard swim, a 10-mile bike ride and a 1.5-mile run. I knew I could handle all three races. But I had never tried all three in the same day. I don't think Colton, Zach and Tyler wanted to discourage me in case I couldn't do it.

"Do you have your goggles?" Colton asked.

"Yep," I barked.

"OK, let's get you registered and in line to start the swim," Colton said.

We stood in line for what seemed like two hours before I got my paw stamped with a special triathlon stamp. After that, we were guided to the starting line and asked to line up in a sideways line.

"Once you hear the whistle, C," Tyler said, "Sprint as fast as you can, dive in the water, then flip over on your back and do your thing."

"I am ready," I howled.

The whistle blew, I ran as fast I could and did my best doggy dive off the dock. I hit the water, flipped over and saw that I was in...last place. How could this be?

"Go, Celtic!" I heard the Mama yell.

"Come on C-Dog," I heard Dad scream.

I started doing the backstroke as fast as I could. My back paws were kicking and my tail acted like a propeller as it steered me through a huge group of dogs.

"That's it, C," I heard Colton yell. "You are gaining on all of them. Keep going."

I looked around and saw most of the other dogs were doing the backstroke as well. They had more experience than me, but I had more strength than most of them. I had to remember to thank Zach for making me pump iron.

A lot of the dogs were doing the "Doggy Paddle." They were falling further and further behind. I had to remember to thank Tyler for helping me ditch the "Doggy Paddle."

About halfway across the water, I felt a tug in my stomach.

"You might get a stitch," I remember my Grandpa saying. "If that happens, push out hard and it will go away."

I tried it, and it worked!

"Man," I thought. "I am so ready for this race."

By the time I made it to the other side of the lake, I realized I was in fifth place. The dog who looked like Ziggy was way ahead, then there was a group of four of us all bunched together.

"OK," I thought, "it is time to make up some ground on little Ziggy."

I grabbed my bike from Colton, handed him my goggles, and took off on the bike. I was pedaling so fast that I forgot that I had to lean a certain way to steer. I ran right into the back of another dog.

"Sorry," I said as we both got up and dusted ourselves off. "It won't happen again."

The other dog stuck out his tongue and took off. I did a belly flop on my bike and I was right behind him. I caught up with him in no time and let out a big "Rup" as I flew past him.

Now, I had my sights set on little Ziggy. But he was fast on the bike, too. He was amazing. It was going to take something extra special for me to beat this little guy.

"Pedal faster," Colton yelled as we came to a stretch in the road where people could see us. "You are doing great, C. But you have to give it everything you've got."

I was giving it everything I had. But I wasn't going to catch him on the bike. Maybe all the sprints I did with Grandpa would pay off in the run.

Come on, C, Colton said as I handed him my bike at the end of the ride. You have 1 miles left to catch that little guy. You can do it. You can win this thing. I know it.

I took off like a bolt of lightning, and, surprisingly, caught up to the little Ziggy very fast. I was screaming inside.

"I am going to win," I kept telling myself. "My family is going to be so proud of me. I am going to win."

I blew past little Ziggy and continued to widen the lead for about another half-mile. But then I started to feel tired. My legs got heavy. My tongue started to drag on the ground. I needed water. I needed to lay down. I needed to rest.

"Don't stop now, C," Tyler pleaded. "You are doing great. Suck it up. You only have one mile left."

That last mile felt like I was running with a ton of bricks on my back. I had managed to hold off little Ziggy, but he was gaining on me. I could see him getting closer and closer and I simply had nothing left. He passed me about two blocks before the finish line. I had to settle for second.

"It's your first time, C," Colton said, trying to console me. "You did great."

"Yea Celtic," The Mama added. "We are all so proud of you."

But I wasn't proud of myself. I lost. I don't like losing. I felt like I had let the whole family down. I was sick to my stomach.

What's This?

I couldn't even look at my family as we rode home from the triathlon. I felt like a failure. I couldn't get it through my head that finishing second out of 62 dogs was pretty darn good. I lost. In my mind, that made me a loser.

We pulled in the driveway and Tyler grabbed me and carried me into the house. It was great. I was so tired I could barely move. But once we got into the house, I came to life.

"Congratulations," shouted about 10 other dogs and several family members as we walked in.

My family had thrown me a surprise party. They really didn't care if I didn't win.

"There can be only one winner," The Mama told me. "But you were one of 61 other dogs out there giving it everything you had. We are all so proud of you."

"The Mama" then reached into her purse and pulled out a "gold medal."

"You will always be our champion, C," The Mama said as she placed it around my neck. "It doesn't matter what place you come in. As long as you do your best, that is all we can ask."

Taco and Bruiser had come to celebrate with me. My brother and sister, Kobe and Shaq, also were there. My cousins, Benny, Frankie and even crazy Chloe also made an appearance, as well as Harley, Coby, and Parker, and, of course, Ziggy, who had won the Big Dog Division of the triathlon.

This party was the bomb.

"Celtic," Dad yelled over all the barking. "We have to go back to the vet again tomorrow. They want to check your weight."

Bring it on, I thought. I was in the best shape of my life. I was ready to tackle anything. And next year, I am going to win the Doggy Triathlon. You can count on that.

Printed in the United States
By Bookmasters